MICROSAURS

BEWARE THE TINY-SPINO

M13

M13

MICRO

BOYS

MICROSAURS

BEWARE THE TINY-SPINO

DUSTIN HANSEN

Feiwel and Friends
New York

A Feiwel and Friends Book
An Imprint of Macmillan Publishing Group, LLC
175 Fifth Avenue, New York, NY 10010

Our books may be purchased in bulk for promotional, educational, or
business use. Please contact your local bookseller or the Macmillan Corporate
and Premium Sales Department at (800) 221-7945 ext. 5442 or by email at
MacmillanSpecialMarkets@macmillan.com.

Library of Congress Control Number: 2018944941

ISBN 978-1-250-09035-5 (hardcover) / ISBN 978-1-250-09037-9 (ebook)

Book design by Liz Dresner
Feiwel and Friends logo designed by Filomena Tuosto

First edition, 2019

10 9 8 7 6 5 4 3 2 1

mackids.com

For Jack L., Michael L., and Bethani O.
Official honorary members of the IMPA.

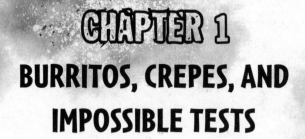

CHAPTER 1
BURRITOS, CREPES, AND IMPOSSIBLE TESTS

Some days you wake up with absolutely nothing to do. You have time to catch up on your comic books. Maybe watch a little TV.

Today was not one of those days.

Before I'd even brushed my teeth, Lin had left me fourteen text messages and three video messages, and nearly worn out the battery on my Invisible Communicator. All because Vicky Van-Varbles, Lin's sworn enemy, had spent the night at her house. A sleepover of epic proportions, and thanks to all the messages, I knew every detail.

After double-checking my backpack for supplies, I bolted out the door and was knocking on Lin's before she could call again.

"Danny, good to see you this fine morning," Lin's dad said as he answered. He was wearing a dish towel around his neck, and he smiled his nice dad smile, which always made me feel good.

"Thanks, Mr. Song. It's nice to see you, too. Is Lin here?" I asked.

"Nope. NASA stopped by this morning and asked her to go on a secret space mission," he said. "She won't be back for twenty-seven years. You just missed her."

"Well, in that case, I guess I can help myself to her video game collection. All the games will be outdated by the time she returns," I said.

Mr. Song stepped out of the doorway and motioned for me to enter. "Help yourself. Oh, and help yourself to some breakfast, too. We've got a special chef in this morning."

No doubt about it, Mr. Song is funny. Of course the NASA story was a joke—nobody goes away for twenty-seven years—but I could tell by the smell in the air the chef thing wasn't. I heard the clink and clang of knives and forks attacking dishes as I made my way into the kitchen.

"Danny! ChuChu wuv Vicky pwapes. YUMMMMY!" Lin's little sister, ChuChu, said from her high chair. Her face was covered in whipped cream, and her hair was slicked back with syrup. Before I could say hello, ChuChu picked up a pancake from her plate and flung it like a Frisbee. It soared an inch above Mrs. Song's head and slapped right to the front of my shirt, where it stuck with a *FLAP!*

"ChuChu!" Lin's mom and dad said at the same time. But I was more interested in the round circle of thin goodness stuck to my shirt. I peeled it off and held it to the light.

"This pancake is so thin I can see through it," I said.

Just then, I noticed Vicky. She was wearing a purple chef's hat with a matching apron. Her name was stitched across the front of the apron in red gems, and she held a pan in a hand covered in a bright purple hot-pad glove. She flicked the pan and one of the thin pancakes did

a perfect flip and landed back in the pan with a sizzle.

"Thanks. They are wonderfully thin if I say so myself. Master Chef Jean-Louise taught me how to make them when I was in Paris last summer on a cooking vacation. Oh, and they aren't pancakes. They are crepes," Vicky said.

"ChuChu wuv pwapes!" ChuChu said again.

"Ohhh! Isn't that the sweetest thing?" Lin's mom said.

"ChuChu wuvs Vicky," ChuChu said.

"Ohhhh! Now *that* is the sweetest thing," Lin's dad said.

"Thanks, Chooch! Vicky wuvs you, too," Vicky said as she slid the crepe from the hot pan to a plate.

I heard a *thunk* and looked over to find Lin. She was sitting next to her mom, and her head was slumped on the table. She groaned.

"Have a seat, Danny," Mrs. Song said. "There's a spot next to Lin. Don't worry. I don't think her morning grumps are contagious."

"Yes they are, Mom," Lin said under her breath as I sat down next to her.

"Danny. Wait until you try these. Vicky made each of us our own special crepe toppings. It's like she can read our minds," Mrs. Song said.

"Mine had cinnamon apples with a hint of spicy pepper."

"It was cayenne, Mrs. Song," Vicky said as she chopped something on the counter behind me.

"And mine was peanut butter and banana," Mr. Song said.

"With nutmeg. Don't forget the nutmeg," Vicky said.

"How could I? It was *magnifique!*" Mr. Song said in a French accent. Then he kissed his fingertips, and everyone except Lin giggled.

"What was on yours?" I asked Lin. I already knew that ChuChu's crepes were strawberry and cream because she was pretty much wearing them at this point.

"Peaches, jalapeños, caramel sauce, with a little bit of whipped cream," Lin said. She looked up at me and rolled her eyes.

"What? Weren't they good?" I asked.

"They were perfect," she said, then thumped her head back to the table again.

"And speaking of perfect," Vicky said, surprising me as she stood behind me with a plate. "Bon appétit!"

She placed the plate down in front of me. Two perfectly rolled-up crepes filled with fluffy white cheese. There were stripes of dark red syrup or something perfectly swirled in curvy lines on top of the crepes.

"What's inside of them?" I asked.

"Take a bite, and then I'll tell you," Vicky said. "Come on. Be adventurous."

I liked the challenge, and the crepes smelled pretty good, so I took Vicky's advice. I took a bite, chewed it a couple of times, then closed my eyes.

"Ham, cream cheese, and green onions. Topped with red-raspberry syrup," Vicky said.

"Oh, gross!" Lin said. "Ham and raspberries? And ONIONS! I think you messed up this time, Vicky."

I opened my eyes, and everyone was staring at me, waiting for me to say something.

"This is the best breakfast I've had in my entire life," I said.

"Of course it is," Vicky said, and Lin opened

her eyes so wide I thought they might fall out and roll onto the floor. "Now, I'll clean up while you finish, Danny. Then it's off to the Microterium. We have a lot to do today."

"You don't need to clean up, Vicky. We'll do it," Lin's mom said.

"What? I have to clean up when I cook," Lin said.

"Vicky is our guest, Lin," Mrs. Song said.

"It's okay. I like cleaning," Vicky said.

"Of course you do," Lin said.

"Well, at least we can help," Mr. Song said as he started adding dishes to the sink.

ChuChu banged her spoon on her high chair. She was obviously finished with breakfast, so Lin used a washcloth to clean her up while we took a few seconds to talk about the day.

"Hey, did you finish your list for the IMPA challenges?" I said.

"My what?" Lin asked.

"The list of challenges to be part of the International Microsaur Protection Agency. You know, so we can convince Vicky to keep this whole thing a secret. That's the entire reason she slept over at your house last night," I said.

"Yeah, I got it. I was up half the night thinking about it. But I started calling the challenge something else," Lin said.

"What have you been calling it?" I asked.

"It's the TROVFPTBACAAMMMLHSIFHTTM list," Lin said, saying every initial.

"I'm afraid to ask, but what does that stand for?" I asked as I shoveled another bit of ham crepe into my mouth.

"Oh. It's my Total Revenge On Vicky For Pretending To Be A Chef Angel And Making My Mom Like Her So I'm Feeding Her To The Microsaurs list. Yours is shorter, though, so let's go with the IMPA," Lin said. "For now, that is."

"Probably a good idea," I said.

"What's a good idea?" Vicky asked as she neatly folded her dish towel and placed it on the counter.

"For us to get going to the Microterium," I said.

"But I need to change first. I can't go like this," Vicky said, motioning to her hat and apron. "I'll be right back."

Vicky ran out of the kitchen, back toward Lin's bedroom. I looked over at Lin and was about to ask a question, but she answered it before I could get a chance.

"Her mom had someone drop off red pajamas, the purple cooking costume, and a few ingredients that we didn't have. And of course, new clothes for today," Lin said.

"Let me guess. Purple," I said.

"Purplish, and very sparkly," Lin said with a grossed-out look on her face.

The door to Lin's room opened, and Vicky was standing there, pulling a bright purple belt around her waist. She was dressed head to toe in her favorite color. Then she pulled on a purple jacket that looked like it had been dipped in glitter. It was so sparkly I had a hard time focusing on it for a minute.

"My goodness, you look adorable," Mrs. Song said. "Lin, doesn't she look adorable?"

"She looks like a frosted cupcake," Lin said.

"I know, right?" Vicky said. Then she did a little twirl.

Mrs. Song clapped, and Lin groaned and rolled her eyes.

Lin snapped on her skateboarding helmet. "Bye, Mom and Dad. We gotta run. We'll be at Penrod's Microterium." As we left, she grabbed a jar with a lid on it from the kitchen table and stuffed it in my backpack. "Come on. Let's go before someone starts picking out the perfect matching fingernail polish to go with a muddy day in the Microterium."

"Wait. Is it going to be muddy?" Vicky said, and I could hear the worry in her voice.

"It's always muddy in the Microterium," I said.

"Be careful," Mr. Song said as we made our way to the door.

"We're always careful. Besides, it's probably more safe than a twenty-seven-year space trip to Mars," Lin said with a grin that told me she enjoyed the joke as much as her dad did.

CHAPTER 2
MAKING PLANS

"Look, all I'm saying is if I knew it was *always* going to be muddy in the Microterium, I wouldn't have worn my brand-new, custom-fitted, limited-edition amethyst Ruby Girls tour jacket," Vicky said as we made our way through the deep grass in Professor Penrod's backyard.

"We aren't going to the mall to get our hair done. We're going to a living Microsaur environment. If it isn't muddy, we're doing something wrong," Lin said.

"I should call my mom and arrange for another outfit," Vicky said.

"Maybe she can bring you something bite-proof, like a suit of armor?" Lin said. I heard her giggle to herself a little.

"Bite-proof?" Vicky said.

I held open the door to the barn-lab, the old

building that worked as a hiding place for the most amazing place on earth, Professor Penrod's Microterium. "Don't worry, Vicky. What you're wearing is just fine."

"Are you sure?" Vicky asked. I nodded, and she smiled at me as she entered. "Thanks, Danny."

The inside of the barn-lab was dark, cool, and familiar. While it was only Vicky's second visit, Lin and I had been there every day since Twiggy, a tiny-dactyl, led us to the mysterious place. Lin marched right past me, heading for the large metal step that acted like a trigger for the Shrink-A-Fier, Professor Penrod's incredible shrinking invention. But I thought it was worth setting down a few rules before we entered.

"Hang on, Lin. Let's go over the plan," I said.

"I know the plan already," Lin said. "Less talk, more action. That's the plan."

"I'd like to hear the plan," Vicky said. "It's always good to be prepared."

"I agree," I said, and Lin gave me a grumpy look. "What? I do agree. I can't help it. I'm a planner."

"Make it quick," Lin said.

"Okay. There are four tasks you need to complete before you can become a member of the IMPA. And it's super important that you are a member, because you have to pass in order to hang out with us in the

Microterium and help us protect the Microsaurs," I said.

"I like this plan already," Vicky said with a grin.

"I like some of it. The four-nearly-impossible-terrifying-death-defying-tasks part sounds pretty good," Lin said.

"The what?" Vicky asked.

"Oh, nothing. Go on, Danny. Tell us the rest of the plan," Lin said.

"So, the four tasks won't be easy, but they are NOT death-defying. There will be a food challenge, a bravery challenge, a quest challenge, and the Promise Keeper's Oath. Which is the most important, because if you take the Promise Keeper's Oath, it means you have to keep the Microsaurs a secret forever," I said.

"Great. I'll do the food challenge first. I've been working on some amazing recipes. Even better than the crepes we had for breakfast. Where is the kitchen in this place?" Vicky said.

Lin walked behind me, unzipped my pack while I was still wearing it, and pulled out the jar she'd put in there earlier. "Oh, there is no kitchen, and you won't need your recipes. And there's another thing. You don't get to pick the order of the challenges. I do."

Vicky looked like she was going to argue for a second, but then she thought better of it.

"Fine. Give me *your* recipe, and I'll do my best. Which we all know is excellent. After all, I went to a cooking camp last year in—"

Lin cut her off. "In Paris. We know already." She pulled a piece of tape off a wide roll on Professor Penrod's workbench and found a black marker in a long drawer. She started writing something on the jar, then kept explaining.

"But since you brought it up, I think we *should* start with the food challenge. It'll be a nice warm-up for the rest of the day," Lin said as she dotted an i, crossed a t. She looked over at Vicky with a smile that made me a little nervous.

"Are you ready?" she asked.

"I'm ready," Vicky said.

"I'm worried," I said.

"Okay, this one should be easy. First, you need to know you won't be making food for us. You'll be making food for the Microsaurs. Pizza and Cornelia, to be exact. All you have to do is feed them one Microbite each."

"That doesn't sound so bad," Vicky said. "I met them yesterday. They're the twin Microsaurus rexes, right?"

I was confused. I thought Lin was going to make things difficult, but feeding a Microbite to the twins was something we did every day.

"That's them. Oh, and I forgot to mention

you'd be wearing this." Lin pulled a small plastic lunch bag out of her back pocket. Inside was a half-smashed, half-eaten corn dog and a slice of pepperoni with two holes punched in it. "A corn-dog hat slathered with loads of mustard, of course, and a pepperoni jacket. I already stabbed the armholes in it for you. Probably not as cool as what the fashion models wear in Paris, but Pizza and Cornelia are going to LOVE it!" Lin said.

"Umm, I don't know if that's a good idea," I said.

"It's a GREAT idea. I'm kind of jealous, actually. It sounds fun. And they are especially hungry in the morning," Lin said.

"Maybe, I, umm . . . I don't know," Vicky said as she took a step back toward the barn-lab door. "Maybe I will just, umm . . . go for now and try this again tomorrow."

"Wait! Don't leave. We won't send you into the T. rexes dressed like a snack," I said.

"But that's the whole challenge part of the challenge," Lin said.

"We can't turn her into lunch," I said.

"Danny, we're all lunch in the Microterium. But you and I know how to stay off the menu. She has to learn how to deal with dangers of the

Microterium one way or another," Lin said.

"I think she can do that without being dressed like the main course. Sorry, Lin, you need to rethink this one," I said. Then I leaned in and whispered into Lin's ear, "Look, we need her to go along with this. If she gets involved and sees how awesome the Microsaurs are, she'll help us keep the secret. That's the plan."

Lin whispered back, "No, the plan was to set up a test so hard that when she fails we get to keep her in a bug jar for the rest of her life."

"I think we have different plans, Lin," I whispered.

"You guys know I can hear you, right? You are both horrible whisperers," Vicky said. "Also, I'm not wearing that stuff. I'm not afraid, I just refuse to wear a greasy glob of carnival food for a hat and a slimy meat coat over my favorite new jacket. No way."

"Fine. We'll go on to the next one while I rethink the food challenge. But this is still part of the deal," Lin said as she spun the jar around, showing us what she had written on the tape. "Come on. It's time to shrink!"

Lin tiptoed into the Microterium, then carefully placed the bug jar down next to the Fruity Stars Lab 3.0. She turned and looked back at us and dusted off her hands.

"I just realized Lin doesn't like me," Vicky said out loud, which I thought might have been a mistake. She looked like she had no idea that anyone on earth, even Lin, didn't like her.

I've known for as long as I can remember. But I did my best to make her feel like everything was going to be fine.

"Don't worry. She's just testing you. I don't think she wants you to get hurt. I just think she wants to see you in a bug jar," I said with a smile as I stepped on the big metal step.

"True. That's pretty much my main goal in life," Lin said as she got on the step with me.

"Great. That's so much better," Vicky said, then joined us on the metal step. The Shrink-A-Fier whirled to life, and in no time, orange liquid bubbled up into the coiled tube that stretched from the tank to the large showerhead above us. Tiny sprinkles floated down, and we began to shrink.

CHAPTER 3 -
THE FIRST OFFICIAL CHALLENGE

After being shrunk to ant size, the three of us raced to the Slide-A-Riffic. It's a contraption I invented that helps us get around the Microterium. It was half roller coaster, half terrifying elevator, and all exciting.

We launched off the big metal step and zoomed down into the Microterium. We zipped

over the tops of the trees, buzzed by a small herd of galloping Micro-gallimimus, then came to a screeching halt right next to the Fruity Stars Lab 3.0. Lin jumped out first. She held out her arms wide, embracing the awesome scene all around us.

"I just LOVE this place!" Lin said, expressing my feelings perfectly.

Vicky was still a little dizzy from the fast ride on the Slide-A-Riffic, but Lin was ready to go.

"All right. Let's get cracking. We have a lot to do today. Here—you'll need this," Lin said as she unstrapped the chin strap from her helmet, then passed it to Vicky.

"Your helmet?" Vicky said. "What for?"

"It'll protect your brain," Lin said. She turned to me. "So, how long will it take us to get to Frank's Bog?"

I was digging through my backpack, looking for a snack to share with Bruno. I was sure he would show up any second. It's almost like he can sense when we entered the Microterium. "Are we traveling by foot or by Microsaur?" I asked without looking up.

"By Microsaur, of course," Lin said.

38

"About twenty minutes, give or take a disaster or two," I said. "Why do you ask?"

"Because, ladies and gentlemen . . ." Lin said. She held a stick like a microphone, talking in a voice like a TV game show announcer. ". . . Frank's Bog is the location of the first official challenge. It's time for the bravery portion of our event."

"What is Frank's Bog?" Vicky asked.

"It's a mucky, swampy place filled with mushrooms, mud, and mayhem," I said.

"And I'm sure you're wondering what Frank's Bog has to do with the bravery challenge?" Lin continued in her announcer voice. "Well, I could tell you the details, but that would foul up the fun. Spoil the surprise. Ruin the rampage, if you will. But I'll give you a hint. The title of this challenge is 'The Taming of Frank-N-Spine,' and it's a doozy."

"What is a Frank-N-Spine?" Vicky asked.

"Frank-N-Spine isn't a what. Frank-N-Spine is a who," I explained.

"And he's the spikiest, slimiest Microsaur in the Microterium, and I've been wanting to try to tame him forever. And it looks like today is the day. Or at least, today is the day you try," Lin said.

"Have you tried to tame him?" Vicky asked.

"Well, I guess we tried. But we haven't even been able to get close to him yet. He's not what you'd call friendly," I said.

"What? I almost touched him last time.

Besides, it's good he isn't tame yet, or it wouldn't be a challenge. Right?" Lin said.

"Yeah, I guess," I said. "But still, it might be too dangerous."

"All she has to do is climb on Frank-N-Spine's back, ride him around the bog until he's tame, then bring him back here to the Fruity Stars Lab 3.0 so he can hang out with us all the time. Easy," Lin said, knowing that it was anything but easy.

I knew it wasn't going to be possible. I mean, Lin is the best Microsaur tamer I've seen in my entire life, and she hasn't been able to do it yet. I was about to ask Lin to change up this challenge when Vicky spoke.

"Let's go. I'm not afraid," she said. Vicky strapped on Lin's helmet, tucked her pant legs into her long socks, and tugged down the sleeves of her sparkly jacket. She stood tall, huffed out a very determined breath, then continued. "Who could be afraid of something named Frank?

Besides, if you almost touched him, Lin, I'm one hundred percent sure that I can climb on and ride him. No problem. After all, I went on a two-week horse riding camp in Wyoming last year, and the cowboy that runs the place said I rode the wildest horse on the whole ranch. Bring on the Spiny Boy. Vicky's got a monster to tame," she said.

Lin blinked, and a tiny smile lifted the corner of her mouth. If I didn't know better, I'd have to say that Lin was the tiniest bit impressed.

"All right, then. If you're sure," I said. "I guess we're heading to the bog."

But before we could start calling for a few Microsaurs to give us a ride, Lin mentioned the other part of the challenge.

"Oh, and, Vicky, I forgot to mention one thing. Before you can try to tame Frank-N-Spine, you have to find him," Lin said.

"That should be easy. He has an entire bog named after him," Vicky said.

"We can find the bog no problem, but for being such a large Microsaur, Frank can be pretty tough to find. He's camouflaged to fit right in," I said.

"Which just makes the challenge more fun," Vicky said. She lifted her chin, put her hands on her hips, and gave us a look so determined that I almost believed she had a chance.

"And more impossible," Lin said. Then she started calling for Zip-Zap.

CHAPTER 4
FRANK'S BOG

Vicky and I rode together on Bruno's wide back as we made our way to Frank's Bog. She was a little nervous at first. She held on so tight around my waist that I could barely breathe. But soon enough she relaxed, and then the questions began. One after another after another.

"How did you teach Bruno how to let you ride him?" Vicky asked.

"I don't know. He always just did it. We kind of learned together, I guess," I explained.

"Can he go any faster? Lin is way ahead of us," she said, which was true. Lin totally left us behind, zooming way ahead on Zip-Zap, giggling and yahooing as she rode her acrobatic Microsaur.

"Nope, this is Bruno's top speed," I said.

"Why do we have to be small to play with the Microsaurs? Do Microsaurs lay eggs? Have you ever fallen off Bruno? Are those real mushrooms? They look huge! Can you drink the water in the Microterium? It looks poisonous to me."

And many, MANY more. Too many to count. Almost too many to answer. I didn't know about Bruno, but by the time we made it to the edge of Frank's Bog, I was exhausted from answering all the questions. But still, it was kind of fun to have someone so curious about the strange and wonderful details inside the Microterium.

Lin was sitting with Zip-Zap beneath a toadstool. "What took you guys so long?" she said with a grin.

"Well, Bruno isn't nearly as fast as your Zop-Zap," Vicky said. "Especially with two riders."

"It's Zip-Zap, and nothing is as fast as her,

right, Zippy?" Lin said as she scratched beneath the purple Microsaur's chin.

"What makes her so fast? Is it her long legs?" Vicky asked, but before I could answer, a massive, rumbling, goobery-sounding burp-growl grabbed our attention.

"What was that?" Vicky asked with her eyes wide open.

"That's just Frank warming up his vocal cords," Lin said. "Just wait until he really roars—it'll knock the curls right out of your hair, Vicky."

For the first time, Vicky got a good look at the muggy bog we were about to enter. "I'm more worried about this swamp ruining my curls. This place is disgusting."

"I think it's beautiful," Lin said as she climbed out from under the toadstool. "Let's go find our monster! You better stay here, Zip-Zap. It's dangerous up ahead."

Lin jumped into the bog, splashing down both feet into the mud. She turned and looked at us with a big

grin and mud dripping from her chin. "See. It's beautiful."

"And dangerous?" Vicky asked, looking at me.

"Very, VERY dangerous," Lin said as she turned her fingers into claws and made her face all snarly.

Vicky looked worried, but I couldn't tell if it was more about the mud and muck, or the dangerous creatures that made the bog their home.

"Look. If you really break it down, the entire Microterium can be dangerous in one way or another. Even the Slide-A-Riffic is pretty dangerous, but we use it every day. Just pay attention to what's around you and you should be fine. And Lin and I will be with you the whole time," I said.

"For sure. I love this boggy soup, and I wouldn't miss you trying to ride Frank-N-Spine for all the cheese in Wisconsin," Lin said.

"You know, France has the best cheese in the

world," Vicky said. "If you're going to make a bargain to get a lot of cheese, it should be French cheese."

I could tell by the way Vicky was talking that she was stalling.

"Not if you ask me. Wisconsin cheese is gooey, and slurpy, just like the mud in this bog. And speaking of this bog, are you two going to just stand there or are you going to follow me?" Lin said as she led us into the bog.

Walking in the bog felt like slopping through a bowl of cereal covered in syrup that had been left out all day. Short clumps of grass and tiny green weeds covered the place, hiding muddy puddles of cold water beneath them that you couldn't even see until your socks were already soaked. Lin and I had explored the place a couple of times before, looking for the source of the massive, rumbling, goobery-sounding, burp-growling Microsaur.

It wasn't a guarantee that we'd even find him. First of all, Frank was camouflaged really well. And secondly, sometimes he was so grumpy when you found him it was better to back away and try again another day.

As we walked deeper into the bog, the growling, burping, slobbering sound happened again. This time, it was louder and closer. So much closer that the sound of it made ripples in the muddy water around us.

"This place is amazing, right?" Lin said as she pulled a mud-slathered foot out of a bog puddle.

I looked at Vicky, expecting her to look worried about Frank's loud roar, but that wasn't the case. Actually, she looked the opposite of worried. Vicky looked excited.

"Whoa. I actually felt him growl. He's

gotta be close," she said. Then she pushed ahead of me and Lin, leading the way toward the noise.

Frank grumble-goober-burp-roared again, and I realized Vicky was right. I could more than just hear his roar; I could feel it rumbling in my chest as well.

The mud puddles and grass were left behind as we entered a sloppy grove of reeds and gigantic mushroom-like flowers the color and shape of a clown's nose. We had to help one another over and through the area, taking turns pushing or pulling one another out of the soupy bog and over large stumps and fallen logs.

As we got closer, the bog grew quiet. The only sound was our gooey footsteps and our heavy breathing. Frank-N-Spine hadn't slurpy-rumble-gargle-roared in a while, and I was beginning to wonder if we'd gone in the wrong direction.

We climbed to the top of a small pile of fallen trees. It was the driest place I could find, and

I knew if I was tired of the mud, Lin and Vicky were, too. We were so tired from the walk, none of us talked as I unzipped my backpack and found a pouch of chewy fruit snacks for each of us. Then I unbuckled my canteen, took a gulp of cool water, and handed it to Vicky and Lin, who each took a big gulp. After we sat for a while and caught our breath, I took a good look around at the lush, gooey bog. It was almost like being on another planet, but it was still very pretty in its own odd, murky way.

Then Vicky spoke, for maybe the first time all day without repeating after someone or asking a question. As she stared into the mud and strange plants in front of us, she simply said, "I thought he'd be ugly, but he is the most beautiful creature I have ever seen."

"Who?" I asked.

Vicky pointed straight ahead, and after a second, I saw something blink. The something

was Frank-N-Spine, a perfectly camouflaged
spinosaurus. He was covered from top to bottom
in mud and what looked like big splotches of
red jelly. The skin around his eyes was puffy

and pink, and his nose was so full of boogers
that two perfectly round snot bubbles appeared,
then popped with every breath. As we watched
in silence, Frank gnawed on one of the bright

clown-nose-red mushrooms, which jiggled like a water balloon ready to burst.

While Vicky might have found him beautiful, I think boogery is the term *I'd* use to describe the spinosaurus. And while he looked calm at the moment, I knew something Vicky didn't. Frank-N-Spine was perhaps the grumpiest and certainly the scariest Microsaur in the Microterium.

CHAPTER 5
HE'S NOT THAT CUDDLY

I handed Vicky a pair of thick leather gloves I pulled from my backpack and gave her the best advice I could think of at the time. "Don't be shy. Just go up there and show Frank-N-Spine who's the boss. Be confident."

"And don't forget to grab his tail and give it a good yank. Microsaurs *love* it when you pull on their tails," Lin said, giving Vicky the worst advice she could think of.

"Right. I'm the boss. Yank his tail. Got it," Vicky said. She tightened the chin strap on Lin's helmet, pulled up the thick leather gloves, and put a serious look on her face.

"Forget the tail-yanking part. Just act in control and smile. A lot. Pretend like he's a big cuddly kitten that just can't wait to see you," I said. "It'll help, I promise."

"Okay. Smile at the beautiful booger kitten with a mouthful of teeth and a row of spines all the way down his back. Got it," Vicky said, her face still very serious. Then she flashed a smile. I had to admit, I was pretty impressed with how hard she was trying at this bravery challenge. It isn't easy to smile at something as terrifying as a spinosaurus with a head cold, but Vicky had it all under control.

Vicky took a step into the bog, toward the nearly hidden Micro-spinosaurus, and the sound of her hiking boots sploshing into the mud caught the beast's attention. His eyes twitched and his nostrils flared as he tried to sniff the air, but it was no use. His nose was so full of slime that there was no way he could get a whiff of us, I was sure of it.

"Here, kitty-kitty," Vicky said. "Does the dino-kitty want a hug?"

Vicky held her arms out wide and kept walking toward Frank. I looked over at Lin, expecting to see her smiling, but she looked more nervous than Vicky, which made *me* more nervous than Lin.

"Franky. It's free hug day. Come get a snuggle," Vicky said. She was trying to sound brave and friendly at the same time, but her voice kept cracking and I could see that she was starting to tremble. I don't care how brave you are, standing in a mud bog while approaching a spinosaurus will give you the shivers.

"I think we should call this off before it goes really bad," I said to Lin.

"Yeah. I didn't think she'd go this far. I expected her to run away screaming at the sight of Frank, to be honest," Lin agreed. "I have to admit, I'm impressed. And if you tell her that, I will never forgive you."

Frank stopped chewing on the odd, round mushroom and turned his head toward Vicky. He slowly grinned, his white teeth shining. It wasn't the kind of grin that made you feel comfy; it was more the kind of grin that makes you feel like you are in loads and LOADS of trouble.

"Hey, guys. It's working," Vicky said as she turned to face us. "Did you see that? He smiled at me."

But before Vicky could turn back to look at the smiling booger-a-saurus, he pounced. In a jump as fast as a blink, Frank-N-Spine was face-to-face with Vicky. Mud and gunk flew through the air, kicked up by his big hind feet. He shoved one slimy right nostril right up against Vicky's bright purplish-pink shirt and snorted.

Frank-N-Spine sniffed, dragging in a big breath. He squinted his eyes, tilted his head, then snuffled again. Then again. Then AGAIN.

Then he just paused, staring off into the bog like he'd just remembered something very important. Then Frank jolted his head forward and let out a sneeze so big it echoed throughout the bog.

Vicky was directly in the path of the sneeze, and she went tumbling backward, helmet over heels through the mud. She ended up right below Lin and me. When she came to a stop, Frank-N-Spine searched around for her, but he couldn't see her. He tilted his head and tried to sniff through his clogged nose again.

Vicky stood up again, and I knew I had to act fast. I quickly crawled down next to her and put my hand on her shoulder. I put my finger to my lips, telling her to keep as quiet as possible.

Don't make a sound, I mouthed.

"Why not?" Vicky whispered back a bit too loud, and Frank tilted his head toward us and squinted his puffy eye to try to see us.

I pointed to the spinosaurus, then held my finger to my lips again.

"But he likes me," Vicky whispered so quiet only I could hear. "I want to try again."

I worried that Vicky's brains had been jumbled

during the sneeze launch. To me it looked like she had barely escaped being a snack. I shook my head and whispered directly in her ear, "We can come back later. Right now, he's just too grumpy."

Vicky watched Frank-N-Spine scan around, his puffy pink eyes too swollen to see us, and she decided to trust me.

After what seemed like forever, Frank-N-Spine lost interest in us and went back to chewing on the big red-clown-nose mushroom, and Vicky and I climbed the little pile of sticks to join Lin.

"That was close," I said quietly.

"Too close," Lin agreed.

"Yeah, but it was pretty cool. Right? Actually, I'd even say it was pretty brave," Vicky said, wiping mud and spino boogies from her forehead.

"Sure. Pretty cool, but unfortunately it wasn't brave enough to pass the test. No IMPA for you.

Guess we better head back to your new home. Otherwise known as the bug jar," Lin said.

"That's not fair. I can totally tame him. It's just that he's too stuffed up to smell that I'm not dangerous. His eyes are so swollen that he can't see it's me. My dad has allergies, too, and while they make him grumpy, he says the best medicine in the world is a hug from the world's greatest hugger." She turned to Lin. "And after the wake-up hug I gave you this morning, we both know exactly who the world's greatest hugger is."

"You two hugged?" I asked, more shocked at this news than I was at just about anything I'd ever experienced in the Microterium. "I guess I should have come over earlier. I would have loved to have seen that in person."

"It was fast. I barely remember it," Lin said.

"That's not true. Nobody forgets a hug from Victoria Van-Varbles," Vicky said. "I'm not done yet. In fact, Frank-N-Kitty and I are just getting started," Vicky said. She stood up and jumped from the stick pile, landing with both feet back in the bog.

She marched right up to Frank-N-Spine, a big smile on her face and her hands outstretched. In typical Vicky fashion, she started to talk. And talk, and talk, and TALK to Frank as she approached him. The Microsaur might not be able to see her or smell her, but he sure could hear her.

"Oh, Franky-Wanky. Do you have the sniffle-wiffles?" she said in a high-pitched voice.

"I think she's lost her marbles," Lin said.

"Come here, you poor wittle baby Microsaur. Do you need a huggy-wuggy?" she said as she got closer to the spinosaurus. Frank was facing her now, ignoring the mushroom he'd been trying to eat as he watched the strange, brightly colored mess of a girl approach him, talking in her sweet, rhyming baby talk.

"Yup. She's lost her marbles. They've rolled to the bottom of the swamp, and we'll never see them again," Lin said, which gave me the giggles.

"Oh, wook at you, you itsy-bitsy sweetie. Vicky knows what you need. You need a great . . ." she said as she took a big step toward Franky, ". . . big . . ." Another step, so close she could almost touch his wrinkly-skin. ". . . HUG!" Vicky shouted as she lunged for Frank-N-Spine.

For a second, maybe two, I thought that it had worked. Frank looked down at the odd critter wrapped around his large back leg. The confused look on his face combined with the half-mud, half-purplish-pink Vicky Van-Varbles clinging to him is one I will never forget. But the moment didn't last long before Frank-N-Spine literally FREAKED OUT!

The fin that had been lying down
his back popped up to attention,
displaying colorful markings and spikes
that looked like a row of spears. He
bucked like a rodeo bull, snarling, kicking,
and spinning around as he tried to free
himself of Vicky's world-class hug. Of course,
at this point, the hug had turned from a loving
feel-better snuggle into a hold-on-for-dear-life
death grip.

But even with her best squeeze, Vicky was
sent flying. She landed with a sploosh, right
in the middle of a footprint-shaped puddle.
Franky slipped in the bog, lost his balance, and
launched himself right into the big red-clown-
nose mushroom, his spiky dorsal fin leading the
way. The moment his fin touched the leathery
skin of the mushroom, the red mushroom top
tore open.

I expected red goo to ooze from the open
rip in the mushroom, but that wasn't the case.
Instead, billions of tiny, bright golden particles
poofed from the hole in the huge fungi. As
the particles from the first mushroom made
contact with the surrounding clown-nose-
shaped mushrooms, they poofed open, too.
One by one all the other mushrooms opened
up and coughed out cloud after cloud of tiny
particles.

Poor Frank-N-Spine was caught right in the
middle of the yellow cloud of mushroom dust.
He sneezed, wheezed, and coughed. In a few
seconds, the cloud had spread to Vicky. She
coughed and tucked her nose and mouth into
the collar of her shirt. Lin sneezed, then rubbed
her nose with the back of her hand. Then all of
a sudden my eyes started to itch, and I sneezed,
too.

Frank-N-Spine ran away from the cloud of golden mushroom dust, and I decided we should do the same. But before we left, I pulled out my camera phone and took a few quick pictures. I had a feeling they would come in handy soon.

CHAPTER 6
THE SNUFFLE CLOUD

We coughed and sneezed our way out of the bog, toward the place where we left Bruno and Zip-Zap. The mushroom dust wasn't bothering us much anymore, but it still floated in the air around us.

"What is that stuff?" Lin asked. "Have you ever seen a plant blow up like that before?"

"I saw something on a documentary one time about jungle plants that do that. They explode, sending bazillions of little seeds everywhere. It's how they survive, but it felt like it was killing us," I said.

"I know, right?" Vicky said. "I was worried there for a moment."

I was about to point out that the air was still thick with golden mushroom dust, when I heard sneezing and coughing up ahead.

"That's Zip-Zap," Lin said, then sprinted toward the noise.

Sure enough, by the time Vicky and I caught up to her, Lin was with Zip-Zap and Bruno. Their eyes were puffy, and their noses were all clogged up just like Frank-N-Spine's. The two helpful Microsaurs were coughing and sneezing so much that the area around them was covered in slime.

"Look what you did, Vicky. You ruined everything!" Lin said.

"No I didn't. I didn't do this. I was only trying to tame the spinosaurus. The rest was an accident," Vicky said.

Bruno sneezed up my back. I turned to look at him, and he smiled like he was happy to share his boogers with me. "Sorry you're sick, buddy," I said. I wiped

a handful of goo off the back of my neck. "Really sorry."

"Well, what do we do now?" Lin asked. "We have to help Zippy and Bruno."

I listened carefully to the marshy woods surrounding us. One thing about being in the Microterium is that, even if you can't see them, there are Microsaurs hiding in the trees and shrubs all around. But even the best hiders in the world have a hard time staying hidden when they are sneezing and coughing. Lin and Vicky were still arguing when I held up my hand to get their attention.

"Wait. Can you hear that?" I asked.

"Hear what? The end of the Microterium as we KNOW IT?!" Lin said dramatically.

"Oh, give me a break," Vicky said, rolling her eyes.

"No. Seriously. Listen for a minute," I said. Much to my surprise, they stopped arguing and listened.

"There is coughing everywhere," Lin said. "They are all sick. Every last Microsaur in the Microterium. We're doomed!"

"Maybe I did ruin everything," Vicky said, and for the first time that day, she looked really worried.

"Maybe?" Lin said. "MAYBE?"

"Before we panic, we need to make a new plan," I said.

"A plan for what? Catching fifty quadzillion microscopic dust particles?" Lin asked.

"That's not even a real number," Vicky said. "But yeah. I think that's what we have to do. We have to catch all this golden dust stuff."

"I don't think we can catch all the particles, but we have to do *something* fast. And I don't think we'll be traveling by Microsaur this time. Bruno and Zip-Zap look worn out. But I have an idea. Follow me," I said.

I led Vicky and Lin through the forest to the river that runs from the bog and ends up pretty close to the Fruity Stars Lab. Part of the river ran underground, and Lin and I had used it to travel once before.

"What are we going to do?" Lin said as Bruno and Zip-Zap joined us at the riverbank. "It's going to take us forever to get back to the lab."

"And even if we do get back to the lab, how are we going to clean all this up? Look, the gold dust cloud is getting thicker," Vicky said. She was right. At this rate, it'd cover the whole Microterium in minutes.

We had to get down the river, and we had to get there fast. I thought about just jumping in and swimming with the current, but there had to be a better way.

"The last time we sailed in this river, we floated on a big egg," I said. "Remember that, Lin?"

"How could I forget? That was Pizza and Cornelia's egg," she said. "Quick. Look around. Find an egg!"

"Does it have to be an egg? Couldn't we just ride a boat down or something?" Vicky asked.

"Sure. Just run to the micro-boat shop and grab one," Lin said.

"Uhh, I don't think the Microterium has one of those, Lin," Vicky said.

"Exactly my point," Lin said.

"Guys! Stop! This isn't helping," I said.

I heard crunching noises to my left and turned to see Bruno trying to wipe his nose on a bush. It wasn't working all that great, but as he brushed his wide head back and forth, I noticed the leaves on the plant were larger than a bathtub. It gave me an idea.

"Hey, you two. See that plant over there? We need five, no six, of the biggest leaves, fast. Bruno will help, but you might need to hang on the leaves until they rip off. You'll have to work together," I said.

"What for?" Vicky asked.

"I think we're going to *make* an egg," Lin said.

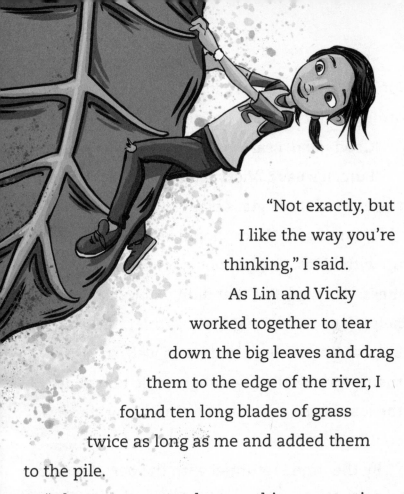

"Not exactly, but
I like the way you're
thinking," I said.

As Lin and Vicky
worked together to tear
down the big leaves and drag
them to the edge of the river, I
found ten long blades of grass
twice as long as me and added them
to the pile.

"Okay, now we need to use this grass to tie
the leaves together," I said.

"We're going to make a boat, right?" Lin asked.

"Yeah, but more like a raft. Or maybe even a
raft train," I said.

"We should braid the grass together into one

long rope. It won't take long, and it'll be much stronger," Vicky said. "I'm an excellent braider."

"Good idea," I said. "Can you show us how?"

"Sure. It's easy," Vicky said as she picked up the ends of three grass blades.

"I'm not sure Vicky should be the one coming up with ideas. Her last one got us in this whole mess," Lin said. But that didn't stop her from helping us braid the grass together. Turns out, Lin was an excellent braider as well, so I let them work on the grass rope while I lined up the leaves and searched for three long sticks we could use as oars.

By the time I returned with the oars, Lin and Vicky had not only made the rope, but they had already started tying the leaves together to make the raft train.

"Is this what you were thinking, Danny?" Lin asked.

"It's perfect," I said.

We finished making the raft train as Bruno
and Zip-Zap lounged on the muddy riverbank,
looking totally worn out. We stepped back to
inspect our work and make sure we had thought
of everything before we pushed off into the
slow-moving river.

"I think this looks more like a canoe train,"
Vicky said.

"Yeah. It kind of does," I said.

"As long as it floats and gets us to the Fruity
Stars Lab soon, I don't care if we call it a banana-
sundae train," Lin said. She stepped in the first
leaf, grabbed her oar, and pushed off into the
river current.

"I'm next!" Vicky said, climbing aboard the
second canoe.

Lin called for Zip-Zap, and the big birdlike
Microsaur jumped into the third leaf canoe. The
braided grass tied to their rafts pulled at the
third, and it started floating out into the river.

"Better hurry, you guys. You don't want to get left behind," Lin said with a grin.

Next up, two leaves were fixed together to make a wide boat, twice the size of the others. "Come on, Bruno. This one's yours," I said. He walked slowly into the river, then pounced on

his leaf raft. It took on a lot of water, but it held him just fine. The last leaf was tied to the end of Bruno's. I grabbed my oar, then ran out into the water and climbed onto my leaf. And just like that, we were on our way to the Fruity Stars Lab 3.0.

CHAPTER 7
AHOY, MATEYS

"Arrgh, this be so relaxing," Lin said in a pirate voice as she lay down in the bottom of her leaf canoe.

"I know. It's almost as good as being in the best spa in France. I've been there, you know. You should really try it out," Vicky said.

"Nar. This pirate prefers chilling in the Microterium," Lin said.

I was standing in my boat, using my oar as a rudder to steer the raft train. Bruno and Zip-Zap were still wheezing and coughing, but it looked like the calm water of the slow river was good for them, too.

"Hey, if you look up into the golden dust, you can make out images. You know, like you do with clouds in the sky," Vicky said.

"Oh yeah," I said as I looked up. "I can see a hot dog with extra mustard."

"Look, look. Right there. It's a kitten chasing a ball of yarn," Vicky said.

"With my good eye—the other is covered in a patch, of course—I spy . . . a bug jar. And guess who's inside?" Lin said.

"Oh boy. I can't imagine who," Vicky said.

"It's you, Vicky," Lin said. "Big shocker, eh?"

"Um, I think there is a bigger shock coming up soon," I said.

"What's that? Is it *you* in the bug jar?" Lin joked.

"No. It's that." I pointed ahead of us. Lin and

Vicky sat up in their rafts and looked. Ahead of us the river was moving faster. Rocks poked out of the river, and white bubbles and foam were crashing up against them.

"Whoa. This slow river looks mad up ahead," Vicky said.

"This is going to be AWESOME!" Lin said, giving up on the pirate talk. She stood up in her boat and grabbed her oar.

Our raft train started picking up speed as we left behind the slow, peaceful water and entered into the rapids. Bruno and Zip-Zap looked nervous, Vicky had no idea how to control her boat, and I was feeling pretty worried myself, but Lin looked totally under control.

"All right, guys. Listen up. We have to row together, or this could get a little crazy," she said. "Don't get me wrong. I like a little crazy, but I'm not sure Bruno and Zip-Zap are up for swimming in the roaring river right now."

"They're not the only ones," Vicky said.

"When I shout ROW, you paddle with your oar," Lin said.

"Won't that just make us go faster?" I asked.

"Yes, I guess. But it'll help us be in control. That's what we need right now," Lin said. "Let's give it a try."

"Row! Row! Row!" Lin chanted from the front. Each time she shouted, the three of us dipped our oars in the water and pulled it back. It didn't take long for Bruno to figure out what we were doing, and he tipped his long tail in the water and paddled, too.

"Okay. Now when I say LEFT, move your oar to the other side of your boat. Ready?" Lin commanded.

"Row! Row! Row! LEFT!" Lin said. We shifted

to the left, and the boats weaved gracefully around a jagged bunch of rocks. We glided past them, then picked up even more speed as the river began to drop.

"Row! Row! RIGHT! Row! Row! Row! LEFT!" Lin continued to direct us as we rushed down the river. We slipped around rocks. Our boats rocked and bobbed up and down as we smashed into waves and crashed through dips and valleys in the river. Water splashed and covered us,

filling the bottoms of our leaf boats with water.
Bruno's double-leaf raft was so full of water
I was afraid it might sink, and then I heard
something up ahead that *really* made me
nervous. Lin heard it, too.

"Oh YEAH! Here comes the big one!" Lin said.

"The big what?" Vicky asked as she spit water
out of her mouth and pushed her hair back from
her forehead.

"Pull in your oars and hold on tight to your

boats, people. We're going over a waterfall!" Lin shouted.

One by one, our leaf rafts went over the edge of the water, plunging into a dark hole in the earth. Cool water showered down on us, and Zip-Zap's CAW and Lin's YAHOO echoed inside the underground cave the river had taken us to.

"Is everyone all right?" I asked as my boat stopped splashing and rocking in the river.

"I think I am. It's too dark to tell," Vicky said.

Bruno woofed, then blew out a very wet-sounding sneeze. I found a flashlight in my backpack, flicked it on, and shined

it around the inside of the cave. Everyone was soaked, but other than that we all looked fine.

"That was incredible," Lin said. "Have you ever done anything that cool in your whole life?"

"Honestly," Vicky said, thinking for a second before she went on. I shined my light on her face, and she smiled really wide. "No. That was the coolest thing I've ever done in my entire life."

"Even cooler than cooking in Paris?" Lin asked.

"About a bazillion times better, actually," she said. "In fact, I want to do it again."

"I know, right?" Lin shouted. "I LOVE THE MICROTERIUM!" Her voice echoed in the cave.

"ME TOO!" Vicky yelled, and it echoed again.

"ME THREE!" I joined in, and we laughed as it echoed again.

The water slowed down again, and we rolled along in the dark with only my flashlight to see the way. After testing out the echo with a bunch of yells, shouts, and Microsaur sneezes, we discussed different ways we could clean the golden dust out of the air. We thought about using a big fan. We wondered if we could somehow vacuum it out of the air. Vicky even suggested we pack up all the Microsaurs and move them to a new spot while we waited for the dust to settle, but nothing seemed right.

"Hey, what's that up there?" Vicky asked. There was a hissing noise coming from in front of us, and I swung my flashlight forward to have a look.

According to a map that Profess Penrod had drawn in his leather-bound field guide, the underground river curled its way beneath most of the Microterium. It passed through a cave with stalactites dipping from the ceiling and stalagmites rising from the floor. But that wasn't the only thing twisting through the cave. An elaborate system of pipes snaked through the cave, too. Some carried hot water and helped keep the Microterium warm above, and some carried cold water like the one making the hissing sound in front of us.

"It's just a pipe, but it's sprung a leak. It's no big deal," Lin said.

This deep in the cave, the gold dust had thinned out, but it was still visible in the beam of my flashlight as we sailed beneath the leaky pipe. We were already so wet that I barely noticed as it rained down on us, but Vicky noticed more than just the water. She noticed something amazing.

"Whoa, would you look at that?" Vicky said. "Maybe it is a big deal."

"What? I don't see anything," I said.

"Exactly," Vicky said. "The leak in that pipe took all the golden mushroom dust out of the air."

"Holy stromboli. She's right!" Lin said.

The air was clean all around us, and my mind started filling with ideas of how we could fix our

golden dust problem with something as simple as a sprinkler. It looked like we needed a bit of rain to get the mushroom dust under control.

As we continued down the river, the dust

started to come back. The broken pipe had done a great job of cleaning the air from one direction; this dust was coming from somewhere else.

"Oh man. That didn't last long. The sprinkler didn't work after all," Vicky said.

"Actually, I think it did. I also think we're almost to the Fruity Stars Lab," I said.

"How can you tell?" Vicky said. "Everything down here looks the same."

"That looks different to me." I pointed up ahead, but this time I didn't need my flashlight. Golden rays of sunshine poured down through a hole in the ceiling of the cave. A hole that was created by a pack of tiny-raptors not long ago, seconds after twin Microsaurus rexes hatched from the largest egg I'd ever seen.

"That's it!" Lin shouted. "That's our way out! Land ho, Danny!"

"Ahoy, mateys. It's time to set anchor and try

our sea legs onshore once again. Guide us home, Captain," Vicky said, joining in on Lin's pirate speak. Even in the dark, I could see a little smile on Lin's face at being called Captain.

Lin took charge again. She helped us as we row-row-rowed our way to the bank of the river, and the three of us and our trusty but still sick Microsaurs jumped on land again.

CHAPTER 8
SPRINKLER

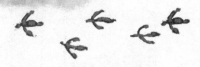

It wasn't easy, but eventually we all climbed out of the underground cave. By the time we reached the surface, all we could hear was coughing and sneezing. And I guess quite a few of the Microsaurs thought that coming to the Fruity Stars Lab was the best way to get help, because the place was surrounded. Squatty ankylosaurs, long-legged gallimimus, a couple of thick-skulled pachycephalosauruses, and more were hanging around, looking miserable with their runny noses and swollen pink eyes.

We didn't waste any time. I started up the Expand-O-Matic as Lin and Vicky ran to the copper penny that worked as a reactor for the Carbonic Expansion Particles. I joined them on the penny, just as the CEPs began sprinkling down.

We expanded, then carefully tiptoed over to

the barn-lab, where I hoped we'd find everything we needed.

"So, this should be pretty easy. We just need to make it rain in here, right?" Lin said.

"Yeah. I think so. But we need to be careful. We need it to rain, but we don't really want to flood the place," I said as I started to consider our options.

"Does Professor Penrod have an automatic sprinkling system? Our gardener installed one at our house, and it keeps things watered even when we're on vacations out of the country," Vicky said.

"No, but that might be something we should talk to him about. The Microterium could totally use a weather system," I said.

"I don't think we have time to make a whole weather system," Lin said. She was right. We needed a quick fix now. I refocused, trying to keep things simple, which was always hard for me.

"So, a hose and a sprinkler, then. Would that work?" Vicky asked.

"Maybe, but the water drops would be pretty big for the tiny dinosaurs. Especially the young ones," I said.

"The Shrink-A-Fier nozzle makes mist. Too bad we can't use that," Lin said.

"Yeah. That's true. But I'm not sure taking that apart right now would be the best idea," I said.

We all started digging through the barn-lab, looking for something to help. I climbed up a ladder and was digging through a box on a high shelf when Vicky shouted.

"Eureka! I found it!" She was holding a box marked *Things that SQUIRT!*

"It's a good start," I said.
"But what's inside?"

Vicky put the box on the
floor, and she and Lin opened
it up.

"No way! This is going to be SO SWEET!" Lin
said as she pulled a huge water squirt cannon
out of the box. "Dibs on this one."

SQUIRT!

Vicky held up two matching water pistols. She spun them on her fingers like an Old West sharpshooter, and grinned. I jumped down from the ladder and pulled out a water cannon for myself.

"It's got a nice-size tank. Good weight-to-strength ratio. Nice hand grip and an easy to refill opening," I said. I looked at the end of my water cannon. "I think if we make a quick adjustment or two, this might just work."

"YES! I knew it! Follow me," Lin said as she ran out of the barn.

I grabbed a pair of pliers from the professor's workbench and ran out the door. Lin was using a hose next to the big barn to fill her toy, while Vicky was practicing taking aim.

"Mine's full. Who's next?" Lin asked.

"Me," Vicky said, and she started filling her pistols.

"Hey, Lin. Squirt me, will ya?" I asked.

"My pleasure," Lin said. She squeezed her trigger and splattered my already-soaked shirt with a steady stream of water. "Gotcha!"

"Yup, just as I thought. Let me see your cannon," I said.

I used the pliers to pinch the squirt nozzle of the cannon nearly closed.

"I wonder why Penrod has these things in the first place?" Lin asked. I handed her modified water cannon back to her.

"Who knows with the professor. He's a surprise a minute," I said. "Squirt me again."

Lin smiled, took aim, and pulled the trigger. This time she sprayed me with a fine mist.

"Oh man," Lin said. "You ruined it."

"Nope. I improved it," I said with a grin. "Now it's an official golden-mushroom-dust remover."

"Oh yeah. Sweet!" Lin said.

I modified Vicky's pistols while she filled my squirt toy with water. After all of us were equipped with golden-mushroom-dust removers, we went back inside the barn-lab and tiptoed around the outside edges of the

Microterium. With the three of us working together, it didn't take long to cover every inch with mist. After we'd finished, we met back in the barn-lab, and I used the pliers to return Professor Penrod's "Things that SQUIRT" toys back to their original working order.

Of course we had to try them out, so a small squirt fight broke out before we put the toys back in their box.

"So, do you think it worked?" Vicky asked.

"Only one way to find out. Let's go back to the Microterium," Lin said.

"Meet you on the metal step," I said.

In a few seconds, the machine whirred to life, and the Carbonic Reduction Particles began to travel up the tube toward the showerhead. In a few more, we were once again the size of ants. Or better yet, the size of a Microsaur.

CHAPTER 9
THE MICROTERIUM PROVIDES

The air smelled wonderful when we returned to the Microterium, all fresh and new. Everything looked washed. Even the plastic PIBB blocks that made up the Fruity Stars Lab 3.0 were sparkling clean. And best yet, not a speck of the golden mushroom dust floated through the air.

"Well, it looks like we saved the day," Vicky
said. "I knew we could do it."

Then, as if in answer to Vicky's claim, Bruno
and Zip-Zap sneezed in a goobery chorus. Then

I heard something wheezing behind me and
turned to see Honk-Honk making her way out of
the forest. She looked just as bad as the rest of
the Microsaurs.

"Nothing is ever that simple in the Microterium," I said with a sigh. "Looks like we still have work to do."

Honk-Honk tried to honk, but she just sounded like a smashed kazoo. The big hadrosaur lumbered right next to Vicky and lowered her head for a hug. Honk-Honk made a cooing sound as Vicky rubbed her cheeks. She tried to honk again, but all that came out was a scratchy blat, followed by a cough.

"Does this one have a name?" Vicky asked as she hugged Honk-Honk's wide nose.

"That's Honk-Honk, but we might need to start calling her Wheeze-Wheeze. We've got to do something for them," Lin said.

She was right. "It's time to call for help," I said as I pulled out my phone and called Professor Penrod. He answered right away.

"Hello, Danny, my boy," he said. His smiling face made me feel a little better immediately.

"Hello, Professor. Where are you?" I said. I expected him to be outside, searching for Microsaurs, but he was inside a large building filled with people.

"We're in the airport. Heading back to the Microterium. We should be there in an hour or two. Speaking of the Microterium, how are things going?" he asked.

I quickly told him everything. How we found Vicky in the Microterium, how she and Lin were forced to have a sleepover to make sure Vicky could keep a secret. We talked about the IMPA, which he loved by the way, and lastly about Frank-N-Spine and the golden mushroom dust, and how we'd figured out how to get rid of the dust, but that the Microsaurs were still sick.

"Oh my. What an adventure," he said. He didn't look the tiniest bit worried about the Microsaurs being sick, which also made me feel a little better.

"You can say that again," I said.

"I would, but I think it'd be better this time if Dr. Carlyle took over," he said, then passed the phone to Dr. Carlyle.

"Oh my. What an adventure," she said, smiling. Bruno snuggled up behind me and

sneezed down my back again. I wiped the back of my neck and saw the look on Dr. Carlyle's face change. "Yikes. That doesn't look good."

"Doesn't feel so great, either," I said.

"So, this mushroom you said exploded. Can you explain it to me?" Dr. Carlyle said.

"I can do better than that. Hang on. I took a picture." I found the picture on my phone and hit the SEND button to fire off a copy to Dr. Carlyle.

"Hmm. Well, I've certainly seen these before.

But it is odd to see them from your tiny point of view. They are HUGE!" Dr. Carlyle said as she studied the picture. "And I see how this could cause serious problems."

Lin pushed up next to me to see the camera phone. "I'll say. Every Microsaur in the entire Microterium is just like Bruno here. Goobery and miserable."

"These mushrooms can release a lot of spores into the air, and they can be pretty bad for birds and reptiles. Most of them will probably have some kind of allergic reaction. I'm guessing it's having the same effect on the Microsaurs," Dr. Carlyle said.

"Are the spores the golden dust stuff?" Vicky asked, squeezing her way into the conversation as well.

"Yes, and nice to meet you, Vicky. I've heard a lot about you already," Dr. Carlyle said. "Welcome to the Microterium."

"Oh my gosh, you're so nice. Thank you. I love it here, and I have so many ideas on how to make it even better," she said.

"Before we start redecorating the place," Lin said, glaring at Vicky, "we need to help these sick Microsaurs. The only way I know how to fix a cold is a big bowl of chicken noodle soup and a long nap."

"Well, those could both help. But we need something stronger than chicken noodle soup. What we really need is a good dose of Dr. Carlyle's Miracle Fog," Dr. Carlyle said.

"Where do we get that?" I asked.

"You don't get it. You make it," she said. "The good news is that everything you need to make my Miracle Fog is found in nature. The bad news is, I'm not sure what you have there in the Microterium."

"I'm sure the Microterium will provide," I heard Professor Penrod say off screen. "What do you need?"

"Well, we need some ginger root," she said.

"There is plenty of it planted around Snow

Lake. I love the stuff, and so do the ankylosaurs," Professor Penrod explained, tilting the phone back.

"And we need some young and tender eucalyptus leaves," she said.

"Oh my. There are tiny banzai eucalyptus trees surrounding Snow Lake as well. I planted them myself. Plenty of eucalyptus. In fact, I think it's a favorite of the pterodactyls," he said.

"Excellent. And I'm guessing you can find the third ingredient in Snow Lake itself. We need some blue algae," Dr. Carlyle said.

"The lake is literally filled with it. And with pliosaurs, but that's another discussion all together," Professor Penrod said.

"Well, it looks like we're heading to Snow Lake," I said.

"Excellent. I'll send the directions on how to prepare the fog before we get on the plane," Dr. Carlyle said.

We all said our good-byes, and in a few seconds, my phone beeped, telling me the recipe for Dr. Carlyle's Miracle Fog had arrived.

"Ooh, good. She sent pictures of the plants, too," I said. Lin and Vicky studied the images along with me.

"What? These are really just plants," Lin said. "Can you make medicine out of plants?"

Ginger Root

Eucalyptus

Blue Algae

"Sure. Like she said. Everything we need is right here in the Microterium," I said.

"Great. Let's go," Vicky said. Bruno sneeze-cough-burped again. It sounded like an underwater volcano exploded. Then the poor puppyish Microsaur sat down in the wet grass and sighed.

I thought for a minute as I read through the ingredients and Dr. Carlyle's notes on where we could find them. Honk-Honk walked around the side of the Fruity Stars Lab. She sneezed, then leaned against the building.

"All right. We need to work together, and we need to do it fast. We need a digger, a climber, and a swimmer," I said. "Which one do you want?"

"I'll climb," Vicky said before Lin got a chance to claim it.

"I guess I'll dig. I've been wet enough today,"
Lin said.

"Okay. I'll swim. The good news is that
everything we need is right around Snow Lake.
The bad news is that we have to run there. I
don't think the Microsaurs are up for the trip,"
I said. Bruno yawned. He flumped over to the
ground and fell asleep in the sunshine.

"Great. Let's go!" Lin said. She took off
running.

"Wait! Lin! It's this way," I said, pointing in the opposite direction.

Lin screeched to a halt, then started running back toward us. "I know that. I was just giving you a head start," she said.

CHAPTER 10

SNOW LAKE

We made our way to Snow Lake. It was called that because it was the coldest lake in the Microterium. Professor Penrod built the lake right over the air condenser, an underground unit that helped keep the temperature in the Microterium at a constant temperature. But the real reason the lake was kept cold was because that is the temperature the pliosaurs liked best. A few degrees above freezing.

Great for pliosaurs, not so great for me.

"Okay, Lin," I said as I tried to catch my breath. "Remember, the ginger plant is long and spiky with a thing that looks like a pinecone on top of it. Professor Penrod said it grows on the banks of Snow Lake, but it might be kind of hard to find. And we don't need the leaves of the plant; we need a big chunk of the roots," I said.

"Wait. I forgot a shovel. What am I supposed to dig with?" Lin asked.

"Uhh, I didn't think of that. I guess with your hands?" I said.

"Awesome. Race ya!" Lin said, then started searching through the grass for the ginger plant.

"Hurry. Point me toward the eucalyptus," Vicky asked. "I want to be back before Lin."

"They grow on that little hill over there." I pointed behind us to a mound of earth topped with a thick forest of bluish-gray banzai trees. "We need the most tender, youngest eucalyptus leaves you can find."

"No problem. I'm on it!" Vicky said. She was about to run, when I stopped her.

"Hang on, there might be a small problem. You'll want to be super careful, because there are a few snippy Microsaurs that live in those trees, too."

"I'm good with snippy. I got this. It sounds easy," Vicky said.

"I've told you this before, but it's true. Nothing is easy in the Microterium," I warned. "Here, take this."

"What is it?" she asked.

"It's a device my dad invented. You put it in your ear, tap it to turn it on, and then just talk like normal. You'll be able to talk to me and Lin from anywhere in the Microterium. It's called an Invisible Communicator," I explained.

"Cool," Vicky said. She slipped the device in her ear, turned it on, and grinned. "Okay, now I'm ready.

"Be careful," I said.

"I will. And don't worry. I'm an excellent tree climber," Vicky said. "Happy swimming."

"Thanks," I said as I left Vicky and ran toward Snow Lake.

I made it to the edge of the lake, peeled off my shoes, and dipped my toe in the lake. It sent a shiver from my foot all the way to the top of my head. Before diving in, I tapped on my Invisible Communicator.

"Can you two hear me?" I asked.

"I can," Lin said. "I found a ginger plant and I'm already digging. I think I should have volunteered to swim. This thing is HUGE!"

"I haven't started climbing trees yet. Still busy climbing the mountain," Vicky said.

"Wait. Vicky has an Invisible Communicator? When did she get one? Now how am I going to tell you secrets, Danny?" Lin said.

"Well, you're already a horrible whisperer," Vicky said. "I don't think this makes a big difference."

"Can we discuss this later? I'm ready to dive in," I said. "I have to leave my communicator with my backpack. Not sure I want to get it wet. So, really what I'm saying is, be nice to each other and hurry!"

I was about to dive in when something tickled my feet. I looked down into the icy cold water and got my first break all day. The shallows of the lake were covered in blue, hairlike strings of algae. I reached down and picked a bunch of it, stuffed my pockets full of the stuff, then slipped the Invisible Communicator back in my ear.

"I'm back!" I said.

"What? That was fast," Lin said.

"And easy, for a change," I said.

"Good. Come help me dig, then," Lin said.

I was about to reply, when a scream stole my attention.

"HELLLLLP MEEEE!" Vicky shouted in our ears so loud it actually hurt. "They are everywhere!"

"The pterodactyls," I said to Lin.

"Yea. And guess who's wearing a sparkly jacket?" Lin said.

"I didn't even think of that! What have we done?"

"We'll dig later. I guess we have to help Vicky."

I started running, but the thought that Lin was willing to help Vicky, rather than let her live the rest of her life stuffed in a bug jar, or worse, be carried away by a glitter-loving pterodactyl, gave me hope as I made my way toward the eucalyptus trees. Who knows, maybe for the second time that day I was about to get a break. Maybe Lin and Vicky could get along after all.

CHAPTER 11
A TREE FULL OF TROUBLE

Lin got to the tree first but not by much. By the time we arrived, there were six small goobery pterodactyls perched on the branches around Vicky, plus one very large pterodactyl named Twiggy, who sneezed loudly from a branch below her.

"When you said banzai tree, I thought it was going to be small," Lin said. "This thing is massive."

"What took you guys so long?" Vicky shouted down at us.

"We got here as fast as we could. I'm coming up to help," I said, then started climbing.

"What can I do?" asked Lin.

"We need a distraction," Vicky shouted. "Every time I pick a leaf, one of these guys steals it from me. Watch!"

Sure enough, Vicky picked one of the tender

eucalyptus leaves, and as soon as it was in her hands, one of the small pterodactyls reached in and snatched it from her.

I was nearly halfway up the tree when I spotted a young leaf close enough to reach. I plucked and held it out. The pterodactyls weren't interested in my leaf at all. I showed it to Lin and called down.

"Just what we thought. This isn't about leaves; it's about sparkles," I said. "Here. Catch." I dropped the leaf, and it floated down to Lin.

"Vicky. Good news, bad news. The good news is, you're an excellent distraction. The bad news is, the pterodactyls don't want your leaves. They want your shiny jacket," Lin shouted up to Vicky.

"Ha. Very funny. Nice try, Lin. There is no way I'm falling for that trick," Vicky said.

"I'm not kidding. Twiggy wants it for her nest. The rest are just there to help her," Lin said.

"Which one is Twiggy?" Vicky asked.

"The big one," I said as I picked another leaf, then another. I dropped them down to Lin.

"Well, there is NO way I'm giving my brand-new, custom-fitted, limited-edition amethyst Ruby Girls tour jacket to a Microsaur!" Vicky shouted. Twiggy took a snip at her, caught the sleeve of her jacket, and gave it a tug. Vicky pulled it back from her and stared the huge pterodactyl in the eyes. "NO WAY!"

"Um, I thought your jacket was purple," I said as I dropped three more leaves.

"Amethyst IS purple, for your information," Vicky said.

"I don't know who is snippier, Vicky or Twiggy," Lin said, and I had to agree she had a point.

I picked a few more leaves, dropped them to Lin, and decided we had enough to make Dr. Carlyle's Miracle Fog. "Vicky. You need to give up your jacket. We have enough leaves for the Fog and we need to make a run for it."

Twiggy sneezed, filling the air around Vicky with a fine mist of Microsaur germs. "I'm coming down, but I'm keeping the jacket," she said. "See you at the bottom, Danny."

Before I could suggest one more time that she leave her jacket behind, Vicky jumped forward and grabbed on to a branch. She pulled herself up to her waist and swung around the branch. Then she let go, did a flip in the air, and grabbed a lower branch on her way down. She swung up, flipped her knees around the branch, and swung around it twice. Next, she did a double backflip to the ground. When she landed, perfectly I might add, she raised her hands above her head and beamed with pride.

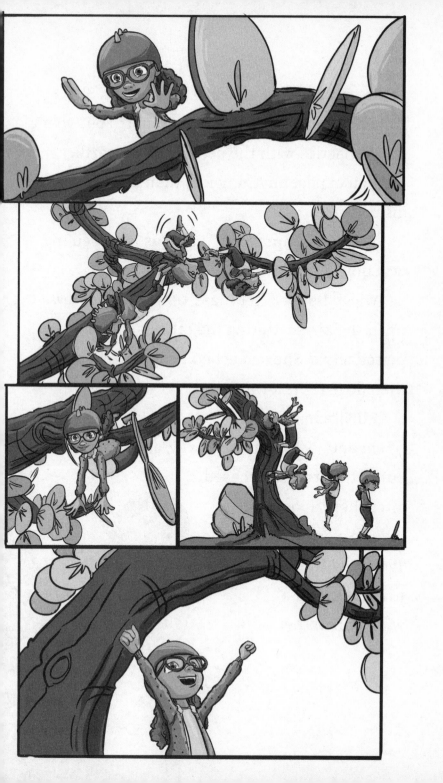

Lin and I looked at her in total shock. She looked back at us and smiled. "What? Four years of gymnastics with the best coach on earth. Did you expect anything less than a perfect dismount?"

"That was impressive," I said as I worked my way quickly down.

Twiggy flapped her massive wings and flew up in the air, scattering the other, smaller pterodactyls. She screeched a high-pitched call, then dove right toward us.

"RUN!" Lin shouted.

Lin and Vicky sprinted away, and I jumped out of the tree and chased after them. I looked over my shoulder and saw Twiggy, with a sparkle in her eye and a wide grin on her

long mouth. She stretched out her massive
clawed feet.

"DUCK!" I shouted as I jumped to the ground.
Lin and Vicky did, too, barely missing Twiggy's

grip. The huge winged Microsaur zipped back up into the sky, turned around as fast as a trickster airplane pilot, then shot toward us again.

Lin dropped some of the leaves, but there was no time to pick them up. We bolted forward, running down the hill as fast as we could. I saw Twiggy's shadow swooping toward us, coming in fast.

"Quick! Under here," Lin said as she jumped beneath a fallen log. Vicky followed her, and I crammed in what was left of the space.

Twiggy flew by us, bolted straight up in the air, then flapped down and landed on the log. Her big toes carved into the wood and flecks of sawdust floated down in front of our eyes. Then she bent over, put her head against the ground, and looked at us upside down and SCREEECHED!

When there wasn't something shiny around that Twiggy wanted, she was as kind as any Microsaur in the Microterium. But when she was eyeballing something she wanted, there was just no way around it, and we all knew it.

"Fine," Vicky said as she took off her jacket. "You can have it. But I want the record to show that I am NOT happy with this decision."

"What record?" Lin asked.

"The IMPA challenge record. This has to count for something," Vicky said.

I had totally forgotten that we were still doing the IMPA challenge. We'd been so busy trying to help the Microsaurs and trying not to get snapped up by Twiggy that it had completely escaped my mind.

"Sure. It'll count. Just give the jacket to her so we can get out of here," Lin said.

Vicky tossed her jacket, and it landed on Twiggy's nose. The Microsaur chirped happily, flapped just far enough away that we could see exactly what she was going to do next but

couldn't reach her, and then she preceded to shred Vicky's brand-new, custom-fitted, limited-edition amethyst Ruby Girls tour jacket.

"Oh, come on. That was just rude," Vicky said. For a second, I thought she was going to cry.

"Well, think of it this way, Vicky. If Twiggy ever has a nest full of baby Twiggys, they'll be wrapped up in your brand-new, custom-fitted, limited-edition amethyst Ruby Girls tour jacket shreds," Lin said.

Vicky smiled a little. She looked over at Lin, and she smiled, too.

"Okay. I'll admit. That is pretty cool," Vicky said.

CHAPTER 12
DR. CARLYLE'S MIRACLE FOG

On the way back to the Fruity Stars Lab 3.0, we stopped and finished digging out the ginger root by the side of Snow Lake. It was by far the heaviest ingredient, and it took all three of us to carry it. As we walked, I read through the instructions Dr. Carlyle gave us for making her Miracle Fog.

"First, we need to smash the ginger root with a mortar and pestle," I said.

"Great. First item on the list and I'm already confused," Lin said.

"A mortar and pestle is a ceramic dish and a smashing tool that you use to, well, smash things," I explained, then kept reading. "Next we need to boil and strain the liquid from the eucalyptus leaves."

"I know how to boil things," Vicky said.

I nodded and went back to the notes. "Then we need to dry the algae and crumble it up into a fine dust."

"How are we going to do that? The stuff is super wet. It's soaking through your pants," Lin said.

"We'll need heat and lots of it. We're going to have to expand to do all this, aren't we?" Vicky said.

"Yes, especially when you read the next part," I said. "Then we measure the ingredients perfectly, add them to a flask and turn them into steam, cool the steam down, and turn it into fog that we can release into the Microterium."

"How in the world do we do that?" Lin asked.

"It is easier than it sounds, but there are a lot of steps and we'll need to be really careful," I said.

"And we still need to hurry," Lin said as we arrived at the lab. Pizza and Cornelia had joined Bruno and the others, and even they were too gooped up and exhausted to chase and play.

"Come on, then. Let's go," I said. I dropped my end of the ginger root and ran toward the lab.

"Don't we need to expand that?" Vicky asked.

"It's already regular-sized. If not, ginger would be the size of a couch in real life," Lin said as she chased after me.

"Oh yeah," Vicky said, then started to laugh. I don't know what was so funny, but something

about a ginger root the size of a couch made us all laugh. In fact, we kept laughing the whole time we expanded, and we didn't stop until we collected our non-couch-sized ginger and found our way to the barn-lab.

It didn't take long to find what we needed to make Dr. Carlyle's Miracle Fog. Professor Penrod's barn-lab was well stocked. Lin started smashing up the ginger root with the mortar and pestle. I showed Vicky how to use the Bunsen burner to boil water in a beaker, and she used that to boil down the eucalyptus leaves into a thick blue-green liquid. And with a little help from an old toaster oven I found under the desk, I had the blue algae dry and crispy in less than twenty seconds.

While Vicky carefully measured out the ingredients, Lin found the perfect flask for us to make our steam. I hooked a long, coiled tube to the end of the flask, then passed it through a bucket of cold water, and placed the end of the tube over the edge of the big metal step.

"So, how does this work exactly?" Vicky asked

as Lin turned up the heat on the Bunsen burner, directing the flame on the bottom of the flask of Dr. Carlyle's Miracle Fog solution.

"It's simple, really. The solution heats up to a boil; then the steam has to have somewhere to go because it has expanded. But the steam will still be really hot, until it passes through all these coils down in the cold water bucket. After the steam is cooled, it will flow through the rest of the tube and out into the Microterium. I've turned this fan on to its lowest setting and put it just below the step, and that should help the Fog travel to every little corner of the place in no time," I explained. "It's not perfect, but I think it's going to work just fine."

"I do, too," said Lin. "But I was thinking, it might be really cool to see the Fog from down there." She pointed to the Fruity Stars Lab 3.0.

"You took the words right out of my mouth," I said.

"To the Shrink-A-Fier," Vicky said, and we all made our way to the big metal step.

As the machine whirled to life, I noticed the first little puff of Dr. Carlyle's Miracle Fog escape from the end of the tube. Orange particles swirled around us, and we began to shrink. In less than a second, we were standing on the metal step, rushing toward the Slide-A-Riffic.

As we coasted down the Slide-A-Riffic zip line, we passed over the tops of trees and entered into the Fog that was starting to build up all around.

Lin took in a deep breath and smiled. "This stuff smells really good."

I took a little sniff, then breathed in deep as well.

"I bet the Microsaurs are going to love it," Vicky said. "Let's go check on them."

I could hear some coughing before we even made it all the way to the Fruity Stars Lab 3.0, and I was worried. But when I saw the Microsaurs, I felt much better. Zip-Zap was walking around, flapping her wings, and even doing a couple of hops. Pizza and Cornelia weren't chasing anything around just yet, but they were at least nudging each other with their wide heads and growling a little. And while there was still some coughing, at least the sneezing had stopped.

Bruno was sitting in the grass, sniffing at the Fog as it rolled by. I unzipped my pack, pulled out a jar of peanut butter, and slathered it on a nice, tasty-looking stick.

"Hey, buddy," I said. He looked over at me and sniffed. "You ready for a snack?"

Bruno woofed, then smiled as a big snot bubble popped out of his left nostril. He bounded over to me and took the stick and started munching on it right away.

"He looks a lot better," Lin said.

Honk-Honk let out a half wheeze, half honk. It wasn't great, but it was progress.

"Dr. Carlyle was right. This Fog is a miracle," Vicky said.

"All in all, it's been a pretty good day," Lin said.

"Good, or great?" I asked, because if Lin was feeling great, then I had a serious question for her.

"I'd say great," Lin said. "Most days in the Microterium are great."

"Well, is it great enough to let Vicky pass the IMPA challenge?" I asked. "I know there's still the bug jar over there, but I think she's proved quite a lot."

Lin rubbed her chin and thought hard, but Vicky chimed in before she could answer.

"No way," she said with her hands on her hips and her head held

high. "My dad always says, if you're doing to do a job, do it right."

"Really? You don't think you passed?" I asked. Lin looked at me and shrugged.

"Well, let's see. There was the bravery test, and we all agreed I passed that by facing Twiggy and giving up my brand-new custom-fitted limited-edition amethyst Ruby Girls tour jacket," Vicky said.

"Right. That was pretty brave. Twiggy can even give me the shivers when she's after something shiny," Lin said.

"And then there was the quest challenge. Not sure what you had planned, Lin, but if building a leaf raft, creating a rainstorm, collecting all the ingredients for Dr. Carlyle's Miracle Fog, and helping spread it to the whole Microterium isn't a quest, then I don't know what a quest is," Vicky said.

"She has a point," I said, and Lin nodded.

"Fine. That counts," Lin said.

"But then there is the food challenge, which should have been the easiest of them all, but we didn't really do that, did we?" Vicky said.

"Can we count the crepes you made us for breakfast?" I asked. Lin shook her head.

"I know sometimes ChuChu acts like a Microsaur, but the rule did say that she had to feed real Microsaurs," Lin said.

"Well, then I have an idea. One final challenge before I'm ready for the Promise Keeper's Oath. Lin, I need the pepperoni and corn dog in your back pocket," Vicky said as she held out her hand.

"I'm sure it's pretty smooshed by now," Lin said.

"I'm not sure it'll work.

It looks like Pizza and Cornelia are feeling a little sick still," I said.

"It's not for them, and I need the Expand-O-Matic, Danny. Can you turn that on for me, please?" Vicky asked, taking charge and giving orders, which was something she was very good at.

"Okay. Right away, Captain," I said. I don't know why I did it, but I saluted her before I ran to turn on the expanding machine.

As the machine warmed up, I watched as Lin and Vicky walked toward the big copper penny that worked as a reactor for the Carbonic Expansion Particles that flowed from the Expand-O-Matic. They were laughing and quietly talking to each other. It looked to me like they were starting to become friends. Maybe it was just Dr. Carlyle's Miracle Fog in the air, but I didn't think so. The Microterium has a way of making that happen.

Lin handed Vicky the plastic bag containing the smashed pepperoni and corn dog muck. Vicky took it, emptied it in her hands, and rolled it into a ball that looked like a soggy, not-so-delicious version of the Microbites Lin had invented earlier. She put the tiny ball on the penny and gave me two thumbs-up.

CHAPTER 13

BACK TO THE BOG

Bruno, Zip-Zap, and Honk-Honk were still a little slower than usual, but they seemed to enjoy the walk to Frank's Bog. Vicky and I rode on Bruno again, because Honk-Honk was busy carrying the big glump of food Vicky had just expanded. The Fog was getting thicker and thicker as we made our way into the swampy area, and I had to admit, I was feeling a little nervous. And it didn't help when Vicky started calling for Frank-N-Spine, promising him a nice big dinner.

"Franky-Wanky, I have your dinner-winner, you big muddy kitty-saurus. Come join little Vicky-Wicky and I'll give you a nice helping of yummy smashed corn-dog-and-pepperoni muck. You're going to love it," she said as loud as she could.

We rode the Microsaurs into the bog for

quite a while, Zip-Zap *not* enjoying the mud between her toes at all. We looked and looked, but Frank-N-Spine was nowhere to be found. Eventually, the Microsaurs were so tired of walking in the muck and glop that they gave up.

After sliding off our rides, Lin and I climbed up on a big mushroom and had a rest, but Vicky was determined. She grabbed a big, sloppy armload of the food mush and headed off on her own.

"Vicky. Let's go back. We can do this later," I suggested. "Frank-N-Spine is probably having a nap somewhere."

"We're so close. I'm sure he's around here somewhere," Vicky said. "Can't you almost feel him nearby?"

Vicky took a couple more steps into the muddy bog, then pushed back a tuft of grass that was taller than her head. That's when I noticed

the ripples in the water and the deep growling
sound.

"There he is," Vicky said. "Come on out,
Franky. I brought you a treat."

The big, wide, wart-covered head
of the spinosaurus slowly rose up

from the water. His eyes were still a little pink and puffy, but the goobers around his nose were almost gone. Vicky held out her arms, which

were still full of the meaty treat she'd brought along.

Frank-N-Spine raised to his full height, water running from his head and neck in little rivers. The massive Microsaur scowled down at Vicky and showed her his big, shiny teeth. He growled and lowered his head toward her, and I felt a flutter in my stomach and my heart beat like a drum in my chest.

He got closer and closer, and then he sniffed through his wide nostrils. The smell of mashed pepperoni and soggy corn dog, mixed with the scent of Dr. Carlyle's Miracle Elixir, and I saw something I never thought I'd see in my entire life. I saw a real, friendly, smiling spinosaurus.

Then, much to my surprise, Frank-N-Spine carefully nibbled away at the treat in Vicky's arms.

"There you go, big guy. I told you it was yummy, didn't I?" Vicky said as she rubbed his forehead. The big beast purred as he finished his snack. Then he licked Vicky's arms clean.

"I think he wants some more. Can you two bring some over here? He's pretty fun to feed," Vicky said.

"You don't have to ask me twice," Lin said. She jumped up and grabbed a huge armload of the food gunk from Honk-Honk's back. I followed her, gathering up the rest, then joined her and Vicky next to Frank-N-Spine.

Our big new friend growled and purred and nibbled until every last smudge of the meaty muck was gone. Then he licked our arms, burped, and grinned as he sat in the mud of his bog.

"Okay, okay. I'll admit it. After that, you have definitely passed the IMPA challenge. I mean,

you didn't just feed him; you fed him, helped cure his cold, tamed him, and made him purr like a kitten," Lin said.

"Not bad for a day's work," Vicky said, looking proud as can be.

Just then, my phone rang. It was Professor Penrod, and I could tell by the image on my phone that he and Dr. Carlyle were standing in the barn-lab.

"Hello, Professor Penrod. Hello, Dr. Carlyle. Good to see you are back," I said. Lin and Vicky leaned in and waved at the phone.

"My goodness, you three are a mess," Dr. Carlyle said.

"It happens in the Microterium," Lin said, and we all shared a little laugh.

"The place smells wonderful. I turned off the Bunsen burner. It seems like we have plenty of Fog rolling around down there," Professor Penrod said.

"Yeah, that's a good idea. Are you guys going to enter the Microterium?" Lin asked.

"Are you kidding me?" said Dr. Carlyle. "I can hardly wait!"

"How goes the IMPA challenge?" Penrod asked.

"Almost finished. Vicky only has to recite the Promise Keeper's Oath, and then she's all finished," I said.

"Great. We'll have another helper in the Microterium. I couldn't be more pleased," Professor Penrod said. "Why don't you three meet us at the Fruity Stars Lab 3.0, and we'll witness her taking the oath ourselves. After that, I have a little surprise for all of you."

"Sounds good," I said.

"I love surprises," Lin said.

"Who doesn't?" Vicky asked, and we all laughed.

CHAPTER 14
THE PROMISE KEEPER'S OATH

"I . . . state your name," I said with my hand raised.

Lin and Vicky raised their hands and repeated after me.

"Promise to do my best to look after the Microsaurs," I said.

They followed.

"And to play with them to keep them happy. I promise to give them healthy snacks and to make sure they have plenty of space to roam, shade to sit in, and safe places to have long naps when the day gets long.

"I promise to never, ever, EVER tell anyone about the Microsaurs, because I know that they need our protection," I said.

They repeated the last line, and I dropped my hand.

"Well, that's it. We're official," I said.

Professor Penrod and Dr. Carlyle cheered, and I was glad to hear Bruno, Zip-Zap, and Honk-Honk join in.

"Wait. Does this mean no bug jar?" Vicky asked.

"Well, for now. But I think I'll hang on to it just in case," Lin said with a smirk.

Then Vicky, Lin, and I joined the celebration as well, cheering and dancing on the surface of a huge copper penny.

"Professor Penrod, don't you have something for our newest IMPA members?" Dr. Carlyle asked when the cheering came to an end.

"Good gravy, I nearly forgot," he said. "Stand together, you three. Closer now. That's it."

He dug in his pocket and brought out three small silver items. "Close your eyes, and hold out a hand," he said.

As we stood together, Professor Penrod placed a tiny object in each of our hands. I couldn't wait to see what it was. I nearly peeked, but I resisted.

"Okay. Open your eyes," he said.

I gasped.

"No way," Lin said.

"What is it?" Vicky asked.

"It's an official IMPA pin. Where did you get this, Penny?" Lin asked.

"From the IMPA, of course," the professor said.

"Wait. The IMPA is real?" I asked.

"Of course it is. We thought you knew all along," Dr. Carlyle said.

"We kind of just made it up," Lin said.

"I thought it was just something for fun that you guys did to test me, actually," Vicky said.

"Well, it is fun, that's for sure," Professor Penrod explained. "But I assure you, it is absolutely real. The IMPA has been around for a long, long time," Professor Penrod said. "Longer than you and me, if you can believe that."

"Whoa. My mind is kind of blown right now," I said.

"I might have told you sooner, but in a way, you were being tested as well. Part of being an official IMPA member is sharing the secret with another trusted member. Vicky here was as much a challenge for you as the challenges you set were for her. Having friends in the IMPA is the only way the whole thing works," Professor Penrod said.

"You see, while this is the first Microterium you've visited, it isn't the only one. There are Microteriums all over the world. Thirty-one of them, to be exact. And we all help each other out from time to time. It is why I travel so much, actually. Dr. Carlyle and I are included in the IMPA, the secret group devoted to the protection, discovery, and happiness of the Microsaurs," Professor Penrod said. He pulled back the lapel on his shirt and showed me his silver pin.

Dr. Carlyle rolled up the sleeve of her shirt and showed us her pin. "And today," she said, "we have three new members of our fine society."

I looked at my pin. It was so shiny that it sparkled in the sun. The head of a blue triceratops with green spots smiled on the face of the pin, surrounded by a beautiful ribbon and the words International Microsaurs Protection Agency. Underneath the chin of the triceratops, which I knew had to be Bruno, were two words

I recognized as Professor Penrod's favorites: *Adventure Awaits.*

"Are you serious? Is this for real?" I asked.

"As real as a Microsaur," Professor Penrod said. "Welcome to the club."

We all cheered again. It had been a long day, and it was time for us to get back. Professor Penrod warmed up the Expand-O-Matic. We said our good-byes, and then Lin, Vicky, and I

expanded for the final time that day. But as we grew, I looked at my two friends and knew that it wouldn't be long before we'd be tiny again and working on another big adventure.

A MESSAGE FROM PENROD

"Hello to the newest International Microsaur Protection Agency member, Daniel Hammer! A bit official-sounding, isn't it?

"I must say, it was a treat to see you and Lin in person again. And meeting Vicky was wonderful.

I'm sure she'll be an excellent addition to our Microterium.

"Things around the old place generally look pretty good, but I'm afraid I have some bad news. Don't worry. The Microsaurs are healthy as can be, that isn't the issue.

"But Dr. Carlyle is suggesting some big changes to the Microterium. A new transit system, a repositioning of the Expand-O-Matic, and a fully automatic weather system are first on the to-do list. And that's only the beginning.

"You see, this is why I partnered up with Dr. Carlyle in the first place. I'm great with the Microsaurs themselves, but when it comes to plants, I'm horrid. And as we saw today, that can lead to some pretty serious consequences.

"I'm going to be a busy man for a while, but in the end, I'm convinced it will make the place infinitely better, for us and the Microsaurs.

"I'd love to hear your thoughts on

improvements, Lin's as well. And we both know that Vicky would be happy to lend a hand on the decorating bits. But until we get the Expand-O-Matic put back in place, we won't be shrinking down for a while. Of course, you can bring a magnifying glass and say hello to all your Microsaur friends in the meantime. Just watch where you step, and keep your bright mind dreaming.

"Take care, my friend, and remember. Adventure awaits!"

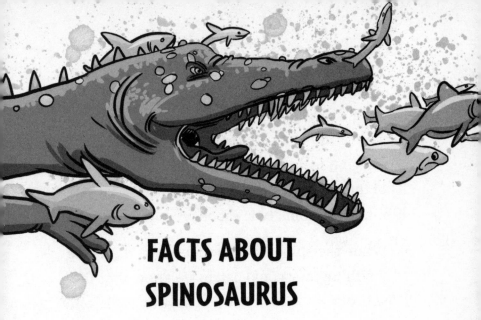

FACTS ABOUT SPINOSAURUS

- There is no doubt where the spinosaurus got their name. The spines on the back of this hundred-million-year-old dinosaur reached over seven feet tall. That's as tall as two third-grade children stacked on top of each other.

- Spinosaurus lived in murky waters, were excellent swimmers, and used their powerful back feet and tail to shoot through the water.

- Scientists believe that the spinosaurus used its spiky sail as a warning to signal intruders. And it was certainly an effective warning at that. Can you imagine seeing a seven-foot spiked sail poke out of the water when you approach a muddy bog? It'd make you think twice about going for a swim.

- While the spinosaurus's menu would include anything they could catch, we know that the sharp teeth, which pointed slightly back, were perfect for catching large mouthfuls of fish, and its lack of molars (chewing teeth) lead scientists to believe that it swallowed a lot of its dinner nearly whole. Bite, tear, gulp!

- And while we often think of the T. rex as being the king of the beasts, there is evidence that the spinosaurus was actually the largest carnivorous dinosaur. Unfortunately, the fossils that have been found of spinosaurus so far are pretty incomplete, so we don't know exactly how big they were, but scientists believe that the spinosaurus could have been as long as fifty-nine feet long and weigh as much as twenty thousand pounds! With teeth like that, that'd make the spinosaurus one seriously terrifying dinosaur.

ACKNOWLEDGMENTS

As always, I'm surrounded and grateful for
the many people who assist in the production
of a book. Top of the list is Holly West, editor
extraordinaire and fellow believer in Microsaurs.
Liz Dresner, purveyor of all artistic things inside
these pages. And the valiant army of editors who
make me look smrt. I mean, smArt. (It happens
more than you can imagine, dear reader.)

And there's no doubt this book would only be a shadow of itself if it weren't for the brilliant third- and fourth-grade students of Ephraim and Manti Elementary. Visiting, laughing, imagining, and plotting with you makes my mind sizzle with new problems (better than ideas, right?). I'll make you a deal. If you keep reading, I'll keep writing.

And lastly, and mostly, I must once again thank my wild family of creative wizards. Here's to making up great stories in life, as well as for the page!

DUSTIN HANSEN, author of *Game On! Video Game History from Pong and Pac-Man to Mario, Minecraft, and More* and the Microsaurs series, was raised in rural Utah. After studying art at Snow College, he began working in the video game industry, where he has been following his passions of art and writing for more than twenty years. Dustin can often be found hiking with his family in the same canyons he grew up in, with a sketchbook in his pocket and a well-stocked backpack over his shoulders.

WATCH OUT FOR

MICROSAURS

TINY-TRICERA TROUBLES

COMING JULY 2019

Thank you for reading this **FEIWEL AND FRIENDS** book.

The friends who made

MICROSAURS

BEWARE THE TINY-SPINO

possible are:

JEAN FEIWEL, Publisher

LIZ SZABLA, Associate Publisher

RICH DEAS, Senior Creative Director

HOLLY WEST, Editor

ANNA ROBERTO, Editor

KAT BRZOZOWSKI, Editor

VAL OTAROD, Associate Editor

ALEXEI ESIKOFF, Senior Managing Editor

RAYMOND ERNESTO COLÓN, Senior Production Manager

ANNA POON, Assistant Editor

EMILY SETTLE, Assistant Editor

LIZ DRESNER, Associate Art Director

STARR BAER, Senior Production Editor

Follow us on Facebook or visit us online at mackids.com.

OUR BOOKS ARE FRIENDS FOR LIFE.

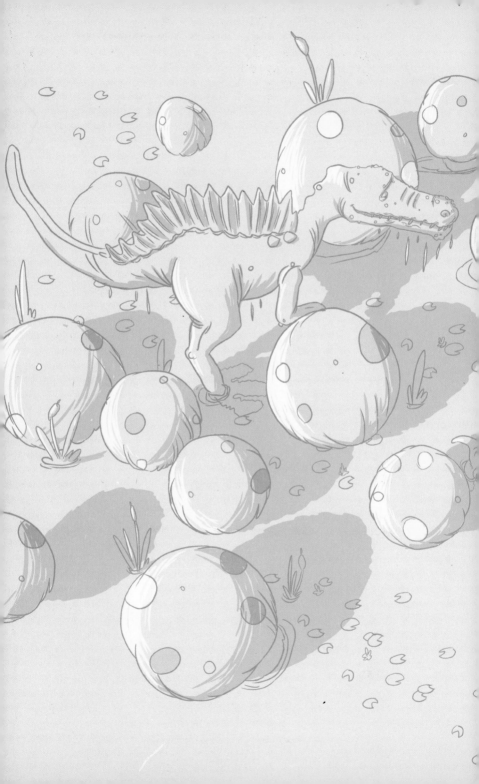